By

Gary Larson

Tom
All Rights Reserved.
Copyright © 2022 Gary Larson
v1.0

This is a work of fiction. Names, characters, businesses, places, events, locales, and incidents are either the products of the author's imagination or used in a fictitious manner. Any resemblance to actual persons, living or dead, or actual events is purely coincidental.

The opinions expressed in this manuscript are solely the opinions of the author and do not represent the opinions or thoughts of the publisher. The author has represented and warranted full ownership and/or legal right to publish all the materials in this book.

This book may not be reproduced, transmitted, or stored in whole or in part by any means, including graphic, electronic, or mechanical without the express written consent of the publisher except in the case of brief quotations embodied in critical articles and reviews.

Outskirts Press, Inc.
http://www.outskirtspress.com

ISBN: 978-1-9772-5221-0

Cover Photo © 2022 Jesse B. Larson. All rights reserved - used with permission.

Outskirts Press and the "OP" logo are trademarks belonging to Outskirts Press, Inc.

PRINTED IN THE UNITED STATES OF AMERICA

PROMOTIONAL BLURBS

Gary Larson, teller of heartfelt stories par excellence, brings to his work a huge soul and an unquenchable desire to share his rich and complex experience. These qualities leap off the page in this moving, tragic yet celebratory account taken almost entirely from real life: a tale that illuminates a remarkable friendship of international reach and profound emotional depth. Once more, Pastor Gary, congratulations and thanks.

> -- Richard Simpson,
> contributing editor,
> *Tar River Poetry*

Immigrants founded America. For centuries they have contributed to our culture, economy, and history. Gary Larson writes from personal experience about the human side of immigration, not the political. A family suddenly must flee their home country to save their lives. After years of repeated displacement and struggle to survive, they finally arrive in America, the land of hope, freedom, and opportunity. Many people welcome them to their new home in small-town America. This is the compelling story of the messy process of trying to fit in, while healing from past wounds. It doesn't always work.

> --Tim Fader, M.D.

This novella strikes something deep in the heart and mind, joyous, sad and yet sweet, and consoles the spirit. It intertwines many aspects of American life that don't receive a lot of attention. Like a tapestry it interweaves the life of a Lutheran Pastor, church work and charity, deep faith and the questioning of that faith. Themes include: American immigration at a very human level, the failures and successes of life, and what we can hope for in a life's continuing journey. It is at times gritty and raw, but at the end hopeful.

> --Edward Hobart
> Tonkin, retired museum
> volunteer manager

If you have ever wondered how life's journey is impacted by unexpected events, faith, and people we meet along our path, this book provides a pantry of reflections to feed your heart and soul. It is a poignant portrayal of lives knit together by nature and faith.

> --Betsy Cashing, School
> of Education, St.
> Bonaventure University

Gary Larson has written a sensitive and thoughtful novella about the long- term effects on people of events which they have no control. Tom is far more damaged than his brother. It falls to Pastor Paul to mentor Tom, leading him to question his faith. A thought-provoking read!

> --Doug Franley, M.D.

PERSONAL NOTES

Thanks to the many who have expressed their appreciation for my first two books which led to the writing of this third. Thanks to my wife, Sarah, and our two sons, Benjamin Larson-Wolbrink and Jesse Larson, who offered their encouragement and assistance. Thanks to my friend and proof-reader, Dean Baldwin, retired English professor at Behrend in Erie, Pennsylvania. Thanks to the powers that be for an exceptionally special friendship between this author and Tom.   Gary Larson

CONTENTS

1. LAO 1
2. PAUL STRAUSSER.................................... 6
3. SPONSORSHIP...12
4. SETTLING IN 16
5. WEDDING 22
6. CHURCH CAMP 26
7. FLISHING...30
8. CUSTODIAN 35
9. BREAKDOWN 40
10. INTERVAL.. 46
11. PRISON 50
12. COVID 59
13. CONSOLATION...................................... 63
QUESTIONS FOR REFLECTION AND DISCUSSION 69

1

LAO

LEI AI PHAOUTTAXAYSY was born into a small village in northern Laos near Luang Prabang, the oldest of four children. In addition to his parents, Lei Ai had two younger sisters and his brother Kahoku, the second born. Villagers were mostly rice farmers. Lei Ai's father, Keo Seng, was a part-time soldier, one of the few people better informed about world events than most others in the area. He was recruited by the Laotian army and the United States military, who were attempting to halt North Vietnam's expansion into northern Laos. His orders were simply to observe Viet Cong movement and report such to his higher command. They issued Keo Seng a rifle and uniform. The villagers were not aware of anything out of the ordinary, even though Keo Seng received occasional visitors. It was his purpose to not unduly alarm any of his family and friends.

A few times, Lei Ai and Kahoku noticed that their father, Keo Seng, met with Lao military and other soldiers, who, as they found out later, were from the United States. They all looked so handsome and important in their uniforms. Their meetings were always in whispers, off to the side. The two young daughters had no understanding of the danger. The two boys would not approach their father with questions. All were busy with school, work in the rice paddies, and tending the family garden. Lee Ai and Kahoku thought of their father as being special and important, a big man in their little village. These men who visited him must be great men. Their father, Keo Seng, was among them.

One day, a group of Viet Cong soldiers stormed into Luang Prabang. The day began as any other but ended in unbelievable horror. There were nearly two dozen soldiers forcing their way into their huts, upsetting tables, throwing chairs, and searching. The wife and children of Keo Seng watched as the Cong entered their home. A few minutes later, they dragged Keo Seng out and threw him to the ground. They held up his Laotian Army uniform for all to see. They screamed, "Traitor, traitor," while dragging him up to a nearby hill. In view of the village, the children's father was pushed down upon his knees. A soldier shot Keo Seng in the head. He sank to the ground, lifeless. Lei Ai stood straight, as did Kahoku. Their little sisters cried. Their mother fell faint. Then, the Viet Cong left.

Some days passed. Father was cremated, but not with the usual Buddhist ceremony. There were no monks nearby to administer the rite. It is beyond Western understanding how important the Buddhist burial ceremony is. It is an understood obligation on the part of a Laotian family, a mandate. The soul, it was thought, could not be released for journey to the next reality without the prayers and chants from Buddhist monks. Keo Seng's ceremony was not going to occur. He would remain in Buddhist "limbo." Many years would pass before a proper ceremony took place.

In just a few days, some from the Lao army arrived and spoke to the family. "You must leave now. You cannot stay. The Cong will return. They will kill all of you. They will kill your children as easily as drinking water. They will throw your dead bodies into the rice paddies. What has happened is just the beginning. They rule by fear. To live, you must leave."

The mother and four children saw the fear in these men's eyes. They had journeyed to Luang Prabang to warn them. The family would be fools to ignore the threat. The solders must know, they thought. Their secure, routine lives were being uprooted before their very eyes. They reasoned that there was no choice. Go or die. They packed up all they could carry in a small push cart, piled what they could upon their backs, and started walking south. Their destination was a Thailand refugee camp they would together occupy for nearly six years! At least there, they might be safe.

After weeks of journey on foot through the forested paths, the family of five displaced fugitives walked through the gate of the refugee camp and into the compound. Someone led them to an open space about ten feet square.

"You will live here."

"But there is nothing here," the mother exclaimed.

She received a curt response. "You are on your own to provide shelter. In three days, we expect food to arrive by air drop."

It wasn't long before this family, like hundreds of others, found the dump, a huge mound of debris and cast-offs. They picked through the rubble, selecting tin for a roof, discarded clothing to wear and for mattresses, and food scraps to eat. Everything was thought of as possible food. Insects were eaten, as were dead animals. Nothing was wasted, including internal organs and bones. This was their new life. Everyone in the camp was out to survive.

The eldest son, Lei Ai, stayed close to mother and daughters to protect them and their few possessions. Kahoku spent his time wandering, stealing, learning. He was to bring home anything he could to help the family live. He encountered some from other countries. After some time, he met a martial arts master who taught him Muay Lao. There was purpose to the study. He learned to kill with his hands, his feet, and the daab. Kahoku received the traditional dragon tattoo on his right thigh, filling the entire leg from his knee to his hip. It was understood what Kahoku had become.

When Kaholu was fourteen years old, he was ready for a man's work. He and another would wait for the dark moon cycle, then swim together across the Mekong River. They hid until their clothing was finally dry, then Kahoku approached a Viet Cong soldier standing guard.

"You got light for cigarette, comrade?" They both lit cigarettes. "Fucking Americans. Try to take country. I kill two of
them," Kahoku bragged.

The Cong, believing his ruse, had to do better. "I kill three
US. Shoot all in head. Cut off penis. Feed to pig."

Both laughed. Quickly they were bonded with each other. They talked for some time, building up a level of comfort.
Then, in an instant, Kahoku swept his left hand over the Cong's
mouth. With his right hand, he plunged his daab straight up between the Cong's ribs and into his heart. He dropped dead in an
instant. Next, the goal of the mission. A pen nearby held several
cows destined for slaughter to feed the Cong platoon. The two
boys led one out, soothing its potential fear with just the right
words and touch. Down to the river they went. The cow walked
into the river as the two boys held tight to the tail. With some
coaxing, the cow swam to the far shore, the boys holding on for
the ride. On the other side of the Mekong they led the cow into
the refugee camp. Food for all. They butchered the beast, and
everyone partook. The boys were heroes.

They had to space this plot out over many weeks before going
at it in a slightly different way. One night, Kahoku went by himself. While knifing the Cong soldier, the Cong's rifle discharged.
The unit came running out. Kahoku raced to get a cow to the
river, where he was on his own. He and the cow started to swim.
Dozens of bullets were fired. He must dive, deep and fast—but
not without first placing into his mouth the little brass Buddha
he wore on a chain around his neck. It seemed he stayed under water for minutes and minutes. When he finally came up to
breathe, he was at the distant shore, too far away for bullets to
hurt. The Buddha had saved him. The Buddha had given him air
to breathe underwater!

Months passed. The struggle to live continued. Even in a refugee camp, love blossoms. Lei Ai met a girl named Dara. Before
long they had a daughter, Channa. One day, they all were surprised when a visitor from the United States came to tell them
they had been approved for sponsorship to the United States. A

Lutheran church in the small town of Oak Grove had selected them. They didn't know who these people were. They only knew that they would be on their way out of their hell to a better life, a safer life. They eagerly made their preparations. A plane would be picking them up at the Bangkok airport in two weeks' time. Lee Ai said goodbye to his mother, brother, and two sisters, not knowing when, if ever, he would see them. The Phaouttaxaysy family was once six strong. Now they would be missing their father and eldest son. Mother cried, knowing she would probably never again see Lei Ai, his new wife, and their child.

The war eventually ended. Thousands of refugees were still in camps, unable to return to their homes, destitute, without proper papers, money or resources. Mother and two daughters, then fourteen and fifteen years old, eventually went to live with a brother-in-law in Laos. Brother Kahoku was left at the refugee camp. Nobody, it seemed, wanted him. It was just the way it was. Perhaps he would be better off there, they thought. He was a grown man at age sixteen, and could take care of himself. It would be almost two more years before the citizens of Oak Grove would gather enough resources to bring him to the United States. God only knows what the lad lived through, alone: the fallout of war, abandoned by his family, and living hand to mouth for seven years on a garbage dump.

2

PAUL STRAUSSER

"WHAT THE SAM Hill! Are you crazy? Why would we want to do that?"

"Well, why not? We're bored silly. It might be fun."

"Fun? Church...fun? You're out of your tree. They're a bunch of hypocrites; that's all there is to it."

"How long has it been since you've been in a church?"

"I expect it's been twenty years."

"Me too. At least that long. Ah, come on. What do we have to lose?"

"Can we get drunk first? I might enjoy it more."

"You're a bird brain. Come on. We'll sneak into the back where we won't be seen. Nobody will know we're there."

"I did hear this Pastor Paul does call it like it is. He doesn't mince words. He's building a reputation in this one-horse town as an independent thinker. Maybe he can preach himself out of a wet paper bag."

"OK. Buy me lunch afterwards? I wonder if anybody goes to church anymore."

The two snuck into Pastor Paul's Lutheran church to find an empty pew in the back. Most of the liturgy had already been said. They were just in time for the scripture reading and sermon. Pastor Paul was not who they had expected he might be. He wasn't just portly. He was fat. Fat and short. Worse, he waved his hands around in an effeminate way. He looked like a fat gay guy. Even so, his voice drew them in. There was something "warm" about it that made one want to listen. He had a welcoming way about him.

Pastor Paul began. "Friends, you know how I question faith. I have opened my soul before you. I struggle to believe. It is so hard."

The two visitors perked up. They were gripped by his honesty. He, as the saying goes, seemed to wear his heart upon his sleeve.

He continued. "So, yet another challenging scripture reading confronts us today. I should be reading the comforting words of scripture. I should be offering you the balm in Gilead, the reassuring words of scripture. Instead, I am taken by the many passages which do not give answers but only raise more questions. Like John Bunyan's 'Pilgrim,' we journey from danger to doubt. Yet, I believe that my journey is your journey, and your journey is mine. Let us hear what the wise man Koheleth wrote centuries before Christ. Here is the philosophical observation from this Old Testament sage. He reflects upon life.

"From Ecclesiastes Chapter 7, verse 15, I read, 'In my life of nothing more than vanity, I have seen everything. There is a righteous man who perishes in his righteousness, and there is the wicked man who prolongs his life in his evil doing.'"

Pastor Paul continued, "Let us pray before Almighty God, before whom no person can hide, before whom all things are known. Let us pray to the God of our Creation, to the Lord who guides our living. Heavenly Father, reveal truth to us, truth upon which we can stand to be confident. Lift us from the mire of confusion into the clarity of your holy light. Amen."

Pastor Paul's eyes were closed for so long the two in the back thought he might have drifted off. But indeed, he was still in prayer.

He began his sermon. "Is this existence the result of a fair and just creation? Is there anything resembling equality within the human species? Is there justice anywhere? Or did God the creator simply mess up, screw up, then walk away? It seems so, doesn't it? Be honest. Have you seen good people die young, and evil people live long and prosper? Yes, you have. Yes, I have. Is it enough to settle on some shallow hope that the good will receive their reward in heaven, and the evil will rot in hell? No! How can our good God create a perfect heaven, then create an imperfect earth? For what purpose? Does he like to see us squirm? Are we like those described by Jonathan Edwards of the Great Awakening who said that we are all 'sinners in the hands of an angry God?'

"We joke to make light of our condition. 'Well, you know. No good deed goes unpunished.' Doesn't it seem that way? Does it seem to you that America, with its big heart, it's passionate desire to help the world, steps into it every time it tries to help? Yes, you know what the 'it' is.

"I knew a Catholic sister who liked to say, 'Them that have, gets.' They do. The rich get more. The poor get less, not just in this nation, but around the globe. The rich get rich on the backs of the poor. Like the slaves who built the pyramids of Egypt, the life of a poor man is worthless. How is that equality in creation? Why is it this way? Do we simply fall back upon Darwin's theory that the fittest survive and too bad for the weak? Is this the way God set up his creation upon earth?"

"There is a solution. The wealthy of earth have enough money to feed, clothe, and house every person on earth. If they did, they would have billions of dollars left over. Why don't they share their wealth? Did God create them with endless greed?

"Thousands of books have been written by thinkers, philosophers, economists, and sociologists who have tried to solve the problem of poverty. They can't. They've tried for not hundreds, but thousands of years. Why can't the problem of poverty be solved, changed for the better? Because God has created this world thus. Matthew 26 records Jesus as saying, 'The poor will be with you always.' Why? Why?"

The two visitors were spellbound. This was not the fluff and puff they remembered hearing during their days in church years ago. This was bold, brazen, brash, reality. It was hard. They were troubled. They weren't sure they had made the right choice going into that church, that day. What were they thinking? Out to have little fun. Then this Pastor Paul chap socks them both on the chin and kicks them in the ass on the way out. They wondered how could he keep a church going, talking like that? That kind of talk doesn't lead parishioners to dig deep into their purses come offering time.

Pastor Paul seemed like a searching man, a hurting man, a broken man. How did he come to be a preacher? Why was he there at that church in their town? Perhaps, Pastor Paul's past could shed some light.

Paul Strausser was the oldest of two boys, who grew up in an American family just like all others in the 1950s. These were the good years, when neighbors were neighbors, the economy strong, church and values were in place. There was decency, respect, common sense.

As a church-going family, they were not surprised when Paul felt he received a call to ministry. He had graduated from college taking several courses in religion. His candidates' committee encouraged him to "discern the call."

He was three years into seminary education when his younger brother, Richie, was in his sophomore year at college. This was at the time of the Vietnam draft lottery. It went as follows. There are 366 possible birth dates in the year. The first dates drawn would be the first of the men to be called into service. If a birth date was, for example, August 5, and that day was the 100th date drawn, all 99 dates drawn before would be called before the person whose birthday was August 5. The lottery. It seemed a fair way to go about it. Paul, being in seminary, would have been exempt anyway, but he drew a 342 out of 366. He would be among the last that would be called, if ever. Richie drew a 37. He was drafted out of college in a few weeks and was headed to boot camp.

It was the height of the Vietnam War. Young American men

were being rushed into service. Richie's mother was on edge with worry knowing that he would be sent to Vietnam. Her husband had died suddenly just a couple years previously. Mrs. Strausser wondered if she could cope with losing her youngest son. Paul reassured her with scripture readings and comforting thoughts. He calmed her down with pastoral techniques he was learning in seminary.

Then, in an instant, Richie was dead. Bam. Pow. Richie was dead! Paul had lost his father when he was only seventeen years old. Now, five years later, his only brother was dead. These were two huge blows which took their toll. His mother and he were crushed with grief like so many families before them, and like so many families yet to lose a son. The usual valorous letter accompanied his body. The customary two soldiers stood at the front door to express America's heartfelt thanks for service and life given. Paul held it all in. He had to. He was on his way to becoming a Lutheran pastor. He had to set an example of faith. He did. He graduated from seminary with honors.

The Rev. Paul Strausser was appointed to his first church. But, underneath the excitement, Pastor Paul was struggling inside over the death of his brother and father. He began losing sleep as he labored over endless questions. "Why did Richie draw such a low lottery number? Why was I spared? Is this what life is, just random chance? What purpose was there to Richie's death?" Pastor Paul was becoming angrier. At board meetings he would explode over insignificant matters. Headaches interrupted his preaching. He was missing meetings and appointments. Before things could get worse, the synod removed him from the charge just as he had finished his second year.

Pastor Paul received counseling and took some "time off." Then he was assigned to his second church. But, the second pastorate went even worse. The synod didn't have to intervene. Pastor Paul went berserk during service one Sunday, throwing bibles and hymnbooks, turning over the communion table, and running out of service in a rage. He was admitted to a psych unit and received intensive therapy for several months. Finally, he seemed to stabilize. He had talked things though, it seemed. He had thought things through, it seemed. Would the synod be ready to take a chance on Pastor Paul again?

But before Pastor Paul would return into service, there was something he felt he needed to do. The idea nagged him night and day. He became convinced that this thing must be done. By then, the Vietnam war was over. Paul would go to Vietnam, to the very village where his brother had been killed. He needed to see. He needed to go. He needed to walk where Richie had walked. He needed to do this thing. He spent two weeks living with the villagers as their guests. He ate their food, observed their daily tasks, smiled with their children. He came to realize that, somehow, they were able to pick up and push on. He thought to himself that if they, who suffered so much, could live again, then so would Pastor Paul. Yes, he had been slammed to the ground. The only good choice was to get back up. So, came a healing, a resolution, an inner peace, at least partially. He returned to the States ready to step into the pulpit again.

But the healthy, financially well-off congregations he briefly enjoyed in his first two assignments, would not be so "plum" a third time. The synod sent him into a rural area, where he was less "mainstream," where his ministry could be monitored. If he fell apart again, it would be easier for the synod to control damage with a smaller congregation. Oak Grove and its 72-member church in a rural county, in an out-there-somewhere state was the assignment Pastor Paul would accept if he wanted to continue in Christian ministry.

3

SPONSORSHIP

LUTHERANS WERE AMONG the first to lead the way to resettle refugees from the Vietnam War into the United States. Other agencies and groupings of concerned people helped. But Lutherans were the pioneers. They became good at it.

In Pastor Paul's third church call to Oak Grove, he seemed to be more settled. Perhaps the counseling had helped. Perhaps his trip to Vietnam had helped. Perhaps continual prayer and the passage of time had helped. He was becoming more mature, grounded, and seasoned. "What doesn't kill you makes you stronger," seemed to be a true saying to describe his life's journey.

Pastor Paul had been reading about the refugee resettlement efforts for some time. Like a burr under his saddle, the call to do something drew him to step up, to do something. It was then he discovered the bios of so many Vietnamese, Laotians, Cambodians, and Thai who assisted America in the Vietnam war effort. Pastor Paul knew that particular war was the least popular ever. That shouldn't mean we should walk away from our allies who risked their lives for us. After any war, there's a lot to clean up. Broken countries and people needed attention.

Families, rather than individuals, were given preference for resettlement. Their adjustment to American culture was thought to be easier for a married couple with children than for an individual. The name Lei Ai Phouttaxaysy came up on his computer screen. Married to Dara. One daughter named Channa. Lei Ai's father fought with the United States military and was killed. The family would be given special consideration in light of the father's sacrifice. His family rose up to the high priority list. At that time, Lei Ai and family were in a refugee camp in Thailand.

Pastor Paul knew the provinciality of Oak Grove. It was not easy being a pastor in this community with many small-minded people. There was a West Virginia mountainmentality in Oak Grove. Folks would literally give the shirts off their backs to those they knew. But strangers were strange to them. Some old-timers were heard to say things like, "We don't like their kind." Yet, there was that handful of progressives, the silent minority, folks who could see beyond their own back yard to the world's needs. They understood that a stranger was nothing more than a friend they hadn't met yet.

Pastor Paul pulled together about a dozen people, including some colleagues from the area community college, for an evening meeting in the church parlor to present the idea. He had prayed for some time in preparation. He knew his words had to be selected carefully. He wanted to appeal to their desire to help their fellows, whomever they might be, wherever they might be. As everybody settled in, he began with these thoughts.

"It's been some years since the Vietnam War has ended. We may think it is all over. But, there's an aftermath of war for us and for those who were in the midst of it. Our job now is to take care of our military men and women who have returned to a country who has given them no welcome back parade. This, of itself, is tragic. But perhaps there is an even greater need. There were thousands of local people in Vietnam and surrounding countries who risked their lives to help America's war effort. Many of those who have survived now languish in refugee camps. Many have been there for years. They are in limbo. They can't return to their own countries. They've no homes to go back to. The only way they can get out of a desperate situation is through sponsorship. We Americans are now presented an opportunity to minister to the widow and orphan as Jesus asked us to do. The downtrodden, homeless, and forgotten, these are the children of God that were and are of particular concern. Are we here in Oak Grove being called to do something to help? Is this our time and opportunity to do something powerful in the name of Jesus Christ? Let us pray."

After prayer, Pastor Paul waited in silence for his words to sink in. A discussion began slowly, which then turned lively. It lasted several hours. All had questions. "What will be required of us? How much will it cost? Aren't there others more skilled than we are to do this? How will the refugees fit into this little town in the middle of nowhere? Do they speak any English? How long will we be expected to care for them? Will they become self-sufficient? Do they really want to come to America?"

More meetings were held. The numbers of people attending grew. There seemed to be more spirit for adventure and service in Oak Grove than Pastor Paul had given them credit for. A few articles were written for the local weekly newspaper. The word was out. Oak Grove would be doing something it had never tried to do before. The "nay-sayers" were silent. They stood by the side while others were eager to help. The momentum grew and so did those who signed on to help with the newly formed Oak Grove Refugee Sponsorship Committee.

The bond deepened among those in this small band. They were not only united in task, but in spirit as well. They were comprised of a mix of Christian denominations and a few from the Jewish faith. Many in Oak Grove were already helping Vietnam vets with contributions and service. It was only a small jump in their thinking to support those others who helped America's war effort. The rightness or wrongness of the conflict seemed unimportant. Assisting those who obeyed the call and saw the front lines of war needed help.

Community fund raisers, church-sponsored dinners, and donation cans at store check-outs all brought in much-needed money. The costs were extensive: airfare, food, housing, clothing, everything needed to support a family being transported from one side of the world to the other. These refugees would be bringing nothing with them but the shirts on their backs.

Finally, all was in place. Pastor Paul gathered the committee again for last details and prayer. "As you bring new life to us, Precious Lord, bring new life to those who have lived years at the very edge of death. Amen." All the paperwork had been submitted. They had received approval to sponsor Lei Ai, Dara, and Channa. All they had to do now was await the arrival of this family and this opportunity. Some on the committee said that they felt like the innkeeper who offered his stable to the holy family years ago in Bethlehem. At least their accommodations would be a step up from a cow shed. As the world turned away, there would be room for them in Oak Grove. They were excited and eager to be the best-ever American hosts.

4

SETTLING IN

WHEN LEI AI, his wife and daughter arrived, the committee was out in full force to welcome them. The refugee sponsorship committee had set up an apartment. It was furnished with donations: chairs, beds, crib, linens, blankets, clothing, toiletries, food, everything that could be thought of. There were pots, pans and dishes, and toys for the baby, now almost two years old. They tried to think of every detail.

The first few nights in Oak Grove, the new family stayed in the large home of a retired couple, George and Maxine Shults. Everybody thought it would be an easier transition if others were around during their first days and nights in a strange new land. English was a struggle, but somehow needs were met. With each passing day, the family seemed more relaxed and curious. They had many, many questions. George and Maxine did their best to answer and explain. Soon they moved to their apartment. It was simply cozy, not too fancy, but certainly better than many. The building was selected with care. Good roof. Good furnace. Within walking distance to all their anticipated needs. The committee checked in with them every day and tried to help out however they could. The committee paid for everything. There were hundreds of details.

Lei Ai was eager to work. He came from an industrious and proud people, the working class of the world. His ancestors dated back to a tribe whose original name meant "land of a million elephants." The elephant was a working beast, and a Laotian was a working man. At first it was washing dishes at Rick's Fine Dining. He mowed lawns and cleaned gutters. He washed cars at Phil's Service Station, taking any job that would bring in money. Many on the refugee sponsorship committee hired him for small jobs around their homes, stacking fire wood, washing windows.

After several months, Lei Ai came to speak with Pastor Paul. "My younger brother, Kahoku, still in reflugee camp, Thailand. You bring him here now Pastor Paul?"

Pastor Paul knew about Kahoku, but he had little hope that our country could sponsor a single man. "We will try, Lei Ai. We will try." Maybe the fact that Kahoku had family in the States would benefit his cause. It was an angle he was willing to explore. Pastor Paul called the committee together again to discuss.

"The Lord is shining his light upon you, dear brethren. Think of what you have done. You have saved a family's life. You have dug deep into your time, talent, and treasure to bring Lei Ai and his family to safety for a new life. He still has a brother in the refugee camp he left behind. He has asked us to bring his younger brother Kahoku to the United States. It will not be easy sponsoring him. We will have to argue his case with National. It will help them all if he is able to come. Are you with me in this? Do we have it in us to reach out one more time? Listen to the Holy Spirit as we pray."

True it was. There was more paperwork, many more phone calls and letters, and verifications of financial support. After close to a year, they saw the green light. Word was sent to the Thai refugee camp that Kahoku would be sponsored into the same town in America where his brother Lei Ai was living. What joy! Kahoku was going to be reunited with part of his family.

Kahoku arrived looking like a deer in the headlights. He seemed afraid. He had fear in his eyes. But, maybe, it wasn't fear. Maybe it was exhaustion and loneliness and hunger. He smiled and hugged his brother, then went to bed for days.

George and Maxine Shults again stepped up to offer their home. His guest hosts gave him food and drink when he'd awaken, but then back to sleep he'd go. It was three days before he began to walk well. His face seemed less drawn. He looked less haggard. He did understand that he was in the presence of friends. That gave him a sense of peace he had not known in seven years. He was now eighteen years old, having spent much of his life eating garbage, truly living day to day.

Such strange new surroundings. A bed not made of straw and rags? Chairs to sit on when dining? Silverware? A toilet! Not a hole in the ground? Everything was new including people with white skin, white faces, and white ways. Could he adjust? It was certainly a better life already. At least his belly was full. He was clean. How glorious to shower oneself every day, and with clean water!

Kahoku, like Lei Ai, was eager to work. He stacked wood. He stained and varnished furniture. He ran errands for others with a used bicycle he was given. He had his own rented room which the committee furnished to meet his needs. Pastor Paul tried to spend as much time as he could with Kahoku to help with his adjustment. He would take Kahoku for lunch at a local restaurant, paying for his meals. They would take walks together. Pastor Paul was planting the seeds of a lasting friendship.

One day, Pastor Paul asked him if he liked to fish? Kahoku smiled. "We go flishing down at liver?"

"Yes, we can do that."

"We go now, Pastor Paul. I catch big flish for you."

It was the first of many, many outings. Pastor Paul was amazed at Kahoku's knowledge. He knew where to fish in the river, where the holes might be, and what fish might be living in those holes. He collected all kinds of bait: leeches, worms, crickets, frogs. Kahoku always caught fish when many times Pastor Paul got "skunked."

How he knew how to do so many things amazed Pastor Paul. One day he went over to Kahoku's rooming house to see on the back porch a big plastic trash can. "What's in there?" he asked.

Kahoku lifted the lid and a stench came out. "Little flish. I make anchovy. Three more day, ready eat. You want come back, eat?"

"Well, no, I don't think so. But thank you very much," Pastor Paul responded with as much grace as he could muster.

Kahoku was quick to learn conversational English, a much better student than his brother Lei Ai. They found out that Kahoku was already reasonably fluent in Vietnamese, Thai, some Mandarin Chinese, and of course English. He seemed to adjust faster. In no time he was using colloquial expressions that others took years to understand. Pastor Paul was tuned into the accent and difficult letter sounds. Fish became "flish." Very became "wery." But, he was stumped for some time over the expression "brake ferd." Eventually he came to understand that Kahoku meant "breakfast."

Kahoku built many friendships among the young and old. He was always nearby, eager to offer a helping hand. His energy was boundless and his skills varied and many. It seemed there was nothing he couldn't do. Early on, when he was meeting with the refugee committee, one fella said, "I'm never going to be able to pronounce your name. I'm calling you Tom." He did, and it stuck. It was, in a sense, a christening, a new name, for a new man, in a new community, with a new life. Kahoku liked his new American name. The name Tom seemed to suit him just fine.

People observed that Tom spent little time with his older brother and his family. Only a few times would he be sitting at their table, nursing a bottle of whiskey and smoking cigarettes with Lei Ai. Many thought it might just be the Laotian way. Others suspected there might be some difficulty between the two brothers.

Lei Ai learned that in a town just north some 45 miles distant, they were hiring painters at a new plant which had just been built. The wages would be substantially better than anything he might earn in Oak Grove. Job security was assured. His family left with little notice nor fanfare. The Refugee Sponsorship committee members were surprised. But that was what the committee had hoped for, after all: independence. They would have liked to have said "farewell" before they left. Even so, the family was not so far away. Many came to visit them in their new town. Tom didn't say a word about his brother's leaving. Over the years, they seldom visited each other. Lei Ai's wife had one more child, then she went to work as a home aide. With both incomes, they were able to buy a house. They had adjusted to and adopted the "American Dream." Although the committee didn't hear from Lei Ai and his family very often, they were pleased with the difference they had made in their lives.

Tom also seemed self-sufficient. Though he was friendly, he was also distant. He seemed to be "out and about" a good amount of the time. Like Lei Ai, he passed his driver's test quickly and soon owned a car—an old car, but a car. He would tell stories of hunting in woods miles away, or going fishing in distant lakes and streams. Always, he brought home food. His many years of living off the land had served him well.

One of his more steady jobs was at an edge-of-town bar. He began washing dishes, but worked himself up to bartending. How he learned that trade, no one seemed to know. Like everything else, he was simply a "jack of all trades." Of course, free drinks were an incentive on the job, but nobody on the sponsorship committee knew anything about that.

It was a working man's bar, a bit rough and tumble. When the boys were well tanked, Busty Barbie would appear with her nightly act. She would flatten an empty beer can between her humongous breasts. That really got the men whooped up. On more than one occasion, Tom was summoned to break up fights. Here he employed techniques learned from Muay Lao. This martial art only intended a kill if the attacker could not be "subdued." Tom used to talk about his many methods to subdue. "Grab man, by side neck. Thumb press on big blood vein. One second man drop like dead. Just somewhere, not dead." After he'd put a few of the fellas into La-la land, he'd care for them as they came around.

He was making friends fast, settling in fast. But not everyone liked this foreigner in their town. Tom was still a stranger. He represented change, as it were, in the "complexion" of Oak Grove. Some just didn't understand why he was living in their town. Did he come to make trouble? Why didn't he live with his own kind somewhere else?

5

WEDDING

PASTOR PAUL CHECKED in with the bride. "Are you all dressed and ready?"

"Yes, I am," responded Becky Johnson.

"Well, I think everyone is here. When you hear the brides-maids' processional, come upstairs. Wait until they're all down front. Then, when the bride's processional begins, you start down the aisle with your father. Remember, walk slowly. Slowly. Let everyone stand to take a good long look at how pretty you are today."

"You're so sweet, Reverend."

Becky was a beauty, indeed, softly stepping upon rose petals the four-year-old flower girl had dropped on the aisle floor. It was a sunny July day, just puffy clouds drifting by. The air was clear. The day was bright. The church was full. It could have been a storybook wedding.

At the front of the chancel stood Pastor Paul, three ushers, the best man and groom. "Go to greet your love," Pastor Paul nudged. There they stood, in perfect innocence, stillness, and reverence. He looked so handsome in his borrowed suit coat, white shirt, and black tie. She looked so beautiful in her white gown and train.

"Dearly beloved," Pastor Paul began. All went smoothly as a hundred other weddings had gone. This one, though, was somehow new and different. Not everyone had met the groom. Many knew little about him. Pastor Paul had practiced his name and honored him with a correct pronunciation. He would not use his American name, Tom, but honored him with his given name. "Kahoku Phaouttaxaysy, wilt thou take this woman to be thy wife…?" Folks in the small town of Oak Grove had never heard a name like that before, certainly not at a Christian church wedding. Nevertheless, all were polite and smiling. The refugee sponsorship committee was there in full force, providing all the love and support they could muster.

"You may now kiss your bride," and so he did. "It is now my distinct privilege to introduce to you, for the first time, Mr. and Mrs. Kahoku Phaouttaxaysy." The customary applause sounded. Down the aisle they walked, as strange a couple as that congregation had ever seen. Becky was lily white, not tanned at all. Her new husband was dark skinned with coal-black straight hair. The iris in his eyes were black as well, a noticeable feature. Never had there been a wedding in Oak Grove of two people who looked so very different, one from the other.

Standing at the receiving line, Becky was busy introducing everyone to her new husband. As people passed by, he shook their hand and said, "Sanks you wery much." After the greetings, the couple went off for a quick spin around the small town of Oak Grove. Becky's brother Tim, the best man, drove his car. The customary "JUST MARRIED" sign was taped to the back window. Tin cans on strings tied to the back bumper gave melody to the event.

The reception was held in the back yard of Mr. and Mrs. Guy Johnson, parents of Becky. There were finger foods and fruit punch, but no alcohol. That would not befit any gathering of the Evangelical Full Gospel tradition. On the surface it was all smiles, but there was underlying tension that afternoon. Rev. Clayton Ernest, the Johnsons' pastor, refused to greet or get near Pastor Paul. Rev. Ernest was fully convinced that in Pastor Paul's Lutheran tradition, Pastor Paul was "not really saved." There was also an awkwardness when Rev. Ernest cornered one of Pastor Paul's flock to offer his spiel. "We have to save that young man, Hohoyah, or whatever his name is. He can't be with a nice Christian girl like Becky and not be saved. What is he anyway? Is he one of those heathen Buddhists, worshipping idols? He just stood up there at the wedding, making a mockery of Jesus. He's probably a communist."

Of course, the whole speech was given within Pastor Paul's earshot. But Pastor Paul had heard it all before. There's no way to argue against ignorance, so he just smiled from a distance. He raised his cup of punch as if to offer a toast. The couple was happy. That was all that mattered.

"Do you have a honeymoon in mind, Kahoku?"

"Pastor Paul, we no money go anywhere. We just happy. Sanks you so much Pastor Paul, you marry Becky and me."

"Listen, I won't take no for an answer. You take this money. Tomorrow you two love birds go out to eat someplace nice. Maybe go to Rick's Fine Dining. Get a good steak dinner and a slice of apple pie with ice cream. Would you do that for me, Kahoku? Would you do that for me, Becky?" Pastor Paul pressed a $40 into his hand and walked away.

"Pastor Paul, good man," Kahoku said to Becky. "Pastor Paul, good man."

Tom came into Becky's life from the other side of the world. They were from two different countries, two different spiritual worlds, two different languages, two people of different traditions, histories, and life stories. Yet they fell in love. It was fully apparent to Pastor Paul that they did love each other deeply. There was a tenderness in their relationship, a courtesy toward each other.

When they first met, Tom was stricken, smitten, and stunned by Becky's innocent beauty. Nothing else came to mind. He pressed his hands together, fingers pointing upward, bowed his head, and whispered, "Namaste." Becky had no idea what that holy word meant. What he was trying to say to her? They both smiled. Becky put her hands together, fingers pointing upward, bowed her head, and whispered back, "Namaste." She did not know the blessing of that ancient Hindu greeting, "I honor the divinity in you." Thus, was the beginning of their love which burned brightly and fast.

They were both quite young, but their youth didn't seem to matter. Cupid had drawn his bow to hit the mark. Their relationship was filled with love. Their courtship lasted only months before their wedding day. After the joy of that blessed day, they moved into a small apartment in the "affordable" side of town to begin home building, life-building, together. Walking through town, holding hands, they looked like any other newly-weds, much in love. Each worked part-time jobs wherever they could find them. They were happy. All of life's good things awaited their futures. Soon Becky was pregnant.

6

CHURCH CAMP

PASTOR PAUL'S FATHER had died suddenly when Paul was just seventeen years old. It was a terrible loss. Paul Strausser had never been so lost in his life, so angry, so broken. His growing-up church and his family thought it might be well if he spent a week at camp the following summer. Off he went, not knowing what to expect. He learned so many things: how to play new games, the joy of singing, how to bravely climb to the top of chapel rock. And, he learned about Moses. Paul carved a walking stick, using it everywhere he went around camp. Of course, in no time the children and counselors were calling him "Moses." At camp he met a middle-aged man, Kosol Watachekarron from Thailand, studying for the ministry at a United States Theological School. Kosol taught the children the "monkey game," which all enjoyed. He had never seen a skunk. So, each night they'd stay awake in Adirondack cabins, waiting quietly with their flashlights. The kids would tire. They would, one by one, climb into their bunks to bed. But Kosol kept watch. Finally, on the last night, the skunk arrived.

"Wake up, children. Wake up."

The flashlights were on the skunk for quite some time as he strolled here and there sniffing, then digging up the ground. Kosol was very happy. It was from Kosol that Paul learned a few Thai words, please and thank you. He learned the universal greeting to women, "Sawadee kop kun krop." How surprised Pastor Paul was while traveling in Sweden many years later, seeing a restaurant named "Sawadee", meaning "welcome." He reflected upon how many people in the world travel or immigrate to new countries. It was becoming a colorful world, indeed. Even in Sweden, there was a Thai restaurant!

Paul Strausser felt close to God that week at camp, close to many of his new friends. When they packed up to go to their homes, Paul didn't want the experience to end. It was a powerful event in his life which planted the seed for his eventual vocation. Many years later, as Pastor Paul pondered, he thought about another Southeastern Asian man, Kahoku. What plans did God have in store for him? What places would he see? What would he become?

Pastor Paul became an ardent believer in the value of Christian church camp. Summer camps were one week long. Pastor Paul signed up scores of children to attend. Some who did came from troubled family settings. Some children were abused. At camp they would be unconditionally loved. At least they would have one week in their lives to know what love without fear felt like. As well, maybe they would come to know God from the Bible studies, games, fellowship, from nature itself. It became the keystone of Pastor Paul's ministry. He was responsible for taking hundreds of adults and children to summer camp. Tom was among those who were introduced to camp.

Tom was talented in so many ways. He fit right in. He was just another counselor with a cabin of kids to care for. One day at camp it was noticed that a huge snapping turtle took up occupancy in the camp pond. Pastor Paul was afraid one of the children might be bitten while swimming.

"You want me take care of turtle, Pastor Paul?" When the children were looking the other way, Pastor Paul passed his hand across his neck in a slicing gesture. One day later, Tom announced to Pastor Paul, "No trouble that turtle anymore. He dead."

"How did you do it. Tom?" Tom was an expert fisherman.

"Flirst I catch blue jill with minnow. Put big hook on strong line. Throw in pond, deep water. Next morning, pull on line. Turtle swallow blue jill and hook. He big one, Pastor Paul. Maybe go 20 pound. I tie rope on leg. Drag him far into wood. He hissing, want to bite me bad. I take big, big stone, very heavy. Throw it hard on turtle back. His shell break. I knife his meat. No trouble that turtle anymore!"

The children played many games, among them a favorite, hide-and-seek. Tom would always be right there in the middle of things but hidden. One time he climbed a tall tree and sat among the leaves, listening to the kids call out, "Come out, Tom. We can't find you." Another time he crawled into a ditch and covered himself with leaves. The children walked up and down the road but never saw him. Pastor Paul's mind traveled back to Tom's past. Could these have been survival skills he had learned when in the refugee camp?

"I wouldn't believe it had I not seen it," Pastor Paul told his parishioners. He was there to witness the event. The children gathered around.

Tom began. "See fly on window. I kill heim. Watch". Tom pulled out his pocket knife to begin carving a tiny bow to which he attached a rubber band. His arrow was a toothpick. He sharpened the point, cutting the opposite end in such a way that it resembled feathers. The fly was buzzing around maybe 10 or 12 feet away. "You watch. Quiet." Tom drew back the tiny bow. The arrow flew, going right through the middle of the fly. The children all looked up into Tom's eyes in wonder. He did things that astounded.

A fellow was fly fishing the pond one day standing on the lawn. Little did he know that behind him, with every back swing of the rod, a golden retriever was jumping up trying to catch the fly on the line. Then, "Yip." He did. The hook went right into the dog's tongue, barb and all. The dog was in pain. Nobody knew what to do. Tom gently approached the dog. He sat down on the grass with the dog's head in his lap. He talked to the dog for some time, then opened his mouth with one hand. The dog was compliant, calm. In one swift twist then another a "yip" from the dog, the hook was out. The retriever ran off wagging his tail.

On hikes, Tom would lead the children to follow turkey trails, crawling upon their bellies to witness the most cautious of all woodland birds. The children would lie there in silence, watching the turkeys strut and peck. He showed them how to track deer, identify snake holes, rabbit nests, find critters in the creek. At night vespers around the camp fire, they wondered at the stars.

The children at camp were only eight or nine years old, "first-timers" as they were called, away from home and parents for the first time in their lives. That was part of the camp experience, to slowly help them grow up. The kids would often be homesick and cry, especially at night. Pastor Paul was making his rounds to each cabin at day's end, checking in quietly to Tom's brood of seven little ducklings. All were still awake but quiet. They were snuggled into their sleeping bags, all except one. Tom sat with the child curled in his lap and arms. The two were leaning against the wall sitting on the bed. Tom was singing a Lao nursery song, stroking the child's hair.

> The sun has set. It go to bed.
> Now you like sun, be sleepy head.
> Daddy near to hold you tight.
> Nothing to fear in his sight.
> So, rest and sleep, little turtle dove
> No fear. No pain. Just love.

One by one the children drifted off to sleep. Tom carried his boy to his bunk, covering him up. "He be OK now, Pastor Paul. I sleep on floor next to him bed."

7

FLISHING

PASTOR PAUL AND Tom became great fishing buddies. Pastor Paul had a small rowboat with a five horsepower kicker. They'd go everywhere to all the area lakes, trailing the boat behind the car. They caught fish, hundreds of them. They fished dozens of lakes together. Tom seemed to have an instinct for knowing where to go. Both were too poor to own a battery "fish finder." They just studied the lay of the land and found the fish. They dreamed of opening a restaurant together. Tom and Paul would fish every morning, clean fish in the early afternoon, take naps, then open up for the evening meal only. They had big dreams together. The details were argued and debated. One day they'd surely do it. It became a fishing ritual to talk about working together, spending life together. "Why not?" Pastor Paul thought to himself. Their relationship was growing closer, day by day. They were becoming pals.

It was on the fishing outings with plenty of time to talk that Pastor Paul learned many things about Tom's past. Tom told him about the awful day when his father, Keo Seng, was assassinated by the Viet Cong. Tom told Pastor Paul that someday he would return to Laos to his home town to give his father and mother proper Buddhist burial ceremonies.

Tom told Pastor Paul about his struggles in the refugee camp. "I lucky learn martial art in reflugee camp. I have dragon tattoo." Tom dropped his slacks to his ankles. There was revealed the large dragon on his right thigh.

Pastor Paul's eyes were fixed. "What's that on your lower leg, Tom?"

"That when Cong bullet hit me. Go right through leg. Much blood come out. But Buddha heal me."

Tom told so many stories Pastor Paul couldn't remember them all. For a young man, Tom seemed to have had the life experience of a person three times his age. When Pastor Paul would come home to tell his wife, Hilda, of the latest story Tom had shared, her response was always disbelief, like the doubting Thomas, inserting his finger into Jesus's side.

Pastor Paul blurted out, "But I saw the dragon, Hilda. I saw the bullet hole scar from both sides of his leg."

"Oh, you say so," Hilda would respond every time. Pastor Paul stopped telling his wife about Tom's stories.

One slow day fishing, Tom said, "You see seagull in sky. I catch. Fix you seagull delight."

"Oh no, Tom, you can't do that," Paul responded.

"You wait see. I get heim for you. Cook seagull delight. You like."

"Tom, maybe you could do that in Laos, but you're in America now. There are laws against that. You just shouldn't do it."

Of course, Pastor Paul knew that no matter how good a cook Tom was, cooked seagull would likely taste like crap. At least that's what he thought.

There was no changing Tom's mind. He had caught a small perch. He hooked it deep, right through the back. He stood up in the small boat to cast the fish far into the sky. The gull dove down but missed it. Tom reeled in to cast again. "I wait till he take it good." Tom released the bail to let the line run. He had eyes like an eagle's. The gull was far beyond what Pastor Paul could see, but Tom cried out, "He got it." He yanked hard on the line. The gull began spinning down like a plane hit in a dogfight. The pole bent hard as Tom reeled. The gull sent out cries of protest. It was a long haul. The gull hit the water flapping his wings, screaming. Finally, he brought it in like a bass beside the boat, grabbing the bird by his neck, holding it up. "Look that, Pastor Paul. Hook heim right in beak."

"Tom, I know you want to cook that bird for me. I'm so sorry to say, but you must let him go." Tom tried one more time to persuade Pastor Paul, but the pastor's stern look finally prevailed. Tom dislodged the hook and threw the gull into the sky. He flew away, cussing the whole way up. Tom sat down in the boat to continue fishing for fish. "You miss out, Pastor Paul. That bird be so yummy. I cook. You no want. So be." They fished in silence for some time.

On another fishing day, while Tom cast a lure, a large cormorant dove down to catch it in mid-air. The bird was hooked badly, fighting with all its strength. As Tom reeled it in, the cormorant was flailing its wings, trying to peck Tom in the face. One swift grab, then Tom had him by the neck. "Now, Muay Lao man, subdue bird." He leaned his arm over the boat to hold the bird under water for some time. It moved less and less. Finally, he pulled it up, limp as a wet rag. Tom removed the hook. Then he grabbed the bird by its feet, shaking it upside down until it vomited water. It started to revive. Tom threw it up into the air. Away it flew. "He no take my bait again," Tom said.

Pastor Paul joked, "You seem to be better at catching birds than you are at catching fish." Both laughed, smiling to each other.

They entered fishing contests together. Hundreds of fish would be tagged, then released into the lake. Both Tom and Pastor Paul caught a couple $25 fish, even one $50 fish over the years they fished the contest. One day, as Pastor Paul was reeling a fish in, they both looked at the tag. It indicated a big prize. Rules stated that the fish had to arrive at the fish station alive. They were miles away. With the little outboard engine, going would be slow.

"Fast, go fast, Pastor Paul."

"It's wide open, Tom, the best I can do."

"If this flish die, you lose prize." They couldn't afford a

bubbler, so Tom was constantly changing the water in the pail for increased aeration. "This flish start to die, I breathe my own air into heim, so live."

"Have faith, Tom," Pastor Paul exhorted.

When they arrived at the fish check station, the fish was fit as a fiddle, swimming in circles in the pail. They checked his numbered tag on the dorsal fin. "Woll, you got a big one, Pastor." He went to the book to check through the numbers. "Let's see here. 3245, here it is. Pastor, you just won yourself $5,000"

Tom jumped up and down, doing some sort of foot-stomping dance. Pastor Paul just said, "I can't believe it; I can't believe it."

"All yours, Pastor Paul, because you good man. Buddha god know."

There was a pause as Pastor Paul reflected. "Let's split it, Tom. You were in the boat too. You helped me get it in."

Tom would absolutely not take any of the prize money. "You give me money, I burn. All yours. You catch flish, not I catch."

What a day! $5000. They were giddy with joy.

Relationships deepen. They evolve so gradually. It takes time to create love. Friendships don't happen instantly, but subtly. One day out upon the water, Tom started calling Pastor Paul "Pop." Pastor Paul hardly took notice of it, until that's what Tom called him every time from then on. Pastor Paul had become "Pop." Pastor Paul and Hilda never had children. It wasn't as if they didn't try. It just didn't happen. But Tom, it seemed, was becoming like the son they never had. Pastor Paul so enjoyed their times together. He was always happy to be with this young man. He was proud of Tom, respected his strength, wisdom, resolve, and just plain grit. Pastor Paul thought of Tom as his son, as Tom thought of Pastor Paul as his "Pop."

When work stood in the way for Pastor Paul, Tom would grab his rod to fish the nearby river. He'd catch walleye, northern pike, bass, even some muskies. His fishing reputation quickly became legend in Oak Grove. As he'd walk through town with a couple 30-inch fish on a stringer, dangling over his shoulder, folks would notice. "Where were you fishing?" they would ask.

He would point his finger out in some distant direction and say, "Out there."

He was a hunter too, bagging small game as well as deer. One bitterly cold November day, Tom came by. "No legal hunt yet. We go flish at liver?"

"Hell yeah, why not," Pastor Paul blurted out, then apologized for his vocabulary.

"I find new hole. I bring food."

"Let's do it," Pastor Paul responded.

Noon rolled around. Both men were getting pretty hungry. As Tom opened his bag, the two men sat down on boulders on the bank. It was as fine a meal as Pastor Paul had ever eaten. Tom had made venison jerky, with a basket of sticky rice. Each grabbed handfuls and ate like barbarians. Tom had a small bottle of rye whiskey. They passed the bottle back and forth between them. It was a glorious day. They became mellow and reflective. They staggered home that day without fish. No matter.

8

CUSTODIAN

JOHN WILEY, A bachelor who had been Grace Lutheran Church's custodian for over twenty years, was a rare find. The cleaning and maintenance of the church were not just a job, but a vocation to John. It was a calling. The church was unable to pay much of a wage, yet John was perfectly contented with what they offered. He lived in a small trailer at the edge of town. Out of the blue, John had a breakdown. Folks were never sure exactly what happened. They took him to a psych unit in a nearly town. Somehow, John broke through security, jumping out a window. He fell four stories to his death.

John Wiley's position at the Lutheran Church would be difficult to fill. The church and community were in mourning. His position lay vacant. Someone very dedicated and skilled would be needed to replace John Wiley.

Pastor Paul did as he always did. He prayed. He consulted his vestry board. Tom's name came up. He seemed a natural. He was, after all, the jack of all trades. Pastor Paul sat down with Tom to discuss the position.

"Tom, these are big shoes to fill. John was loved by so many. We believe you can do it. But we can't pay much for the job. We simply don't have the money. So, if you take this, and a better job comes along, take it. We don't want to hold you back. What do you think Tom?"

Tom didn't hesitate a moment. "I take job, Pastor Paul. I clean like you not see clean. I fix all broke. You see. Church be good. Church look wee-all plitty."

Tom proved his worth. If the congregation had been happy with John Wiley's work, they were greatly pleased with Tom's. The ladies of the church could run their fingers over any surface and not find a speck of dust. He took on projects with his own initiative, painting the restrooms, fixing everything that was broken, mowing the lawn, trimming with edges straight as an arrow. In winter, whenever it snowed, he was shoveling the drive and sidewalks hours before anyone showed up. There was an added bonus.

"I cook lunch for you, all here," Tom announced. There was a part- time secretary, an organist, and others who would come into the church for conversation or business all day long. Once or twice a week, the word would go out that Tom would be cooking that day. Anywhere between a couple people to a dozen would show up. One never knew what Tom was cooking, but it would be yummy. Shrimp scampi, Thai noodles with chicken and vegetables, pork tenderloin with onions, mushrooms, and hot peppers. Many more were the delights Tom served. Those who watched Tom dice and slice vegetables were all amazed at the speed of his knife. He wasn't just a cook. He seemed to have the know-how of a chef. His meals had spices, herbs, garnishes, ingredients which presented all new flavors to the diners. The local Chinese restaurant in town was nothing more than "OK" after folks got a taste of Tom's cooking! Nobody had ever eaten a "Laotian meal" before, not in Oak Grove.

"You want hot: I make hot. You no want hot; I do that." A few were brave enough to try the jalapeno, even the habanero. No one dared try his hottest option. Tom always smiled when he offered that: "You want eat dragon's fire?" He always received a polite "No thank you," all believing they would not have survived the experience. After lunch, everyone chipped in a few bucks. Tom earned much-needed money. It was simply a wonderful season in the life of Grace Lutheran Church. Even those around town would joke, "Grace Lutheran has a CCC – Chinese cooking custodian."

When Tom heard this, he offered defiantly, "I not Chinese. I Lao."

Every Christmas, Pastor Paul would take staff photos to send to parishioners and friends. They would line up on the outside church steps: Pastor Paul, Cindy the secretary, Reggie the organist/choir director, and Tom the custodian. How proudly Tom would stand straight up with perfect posture. He worked for Pastor Paul, he would boast. He was custodian at Grace Lutheran Church, he would tell folks at the bar he tended. He always passed out a photo to everyone he knew, compliments of Pastor Paul's generosity.

One day, Tom came to Pastor Paul with a bad toothache. "Oh, hurt bad. I take hammer, knock tooth out."

"Oh no, Tom. Don't do that. I know the dentist over at Four Mile (the next town just down the road). He'll take a look at you. He'll fix you up."

Dr. McAllister did just that. Tom's teeth were in awful shape, no doubt due to lack of brushing for years. He had a bad abscess which Doc opened up. After a few days of antibiotics, Tom was in the pink once more. In their brief conversation they discovered that they were both hunters, especially going after deer. They became good hunting buddies from that time on. Dr. McAllister fixed his tooth without charge. Another of the area's many good guys.

Tom walked into Pastor Paul's office one day. Pastor Paul could see right away that something important was weighing on his mind.

"We talk, Pastor Paul?"

"Sure, Tom. What's going on?"

"I need go Lao, do Buddhist bury ceremony for parents."

"I thought your mother was still alive, Tom?"

"She alive. Yes. No matter. Father die, never have bury ceremony.

Need Buddhist ceremony for heim. Need for Mother too. She be all set when she die. I have duty. I need do this."

"Well, that's going to be a big expense, Tom. How much do you think the trip will cost? How long do you think you'll be away?"

"Need two weeks. No more. Have to find willage she now live. Most need money for airplane and pay Buddhist monks. Maybe we have big dinner to raise money? I cook?"

"Well, that's a grand idea Tom. But will you have other expenses?"

"Only little more. In city have to pay bribe for protection. When sleep at night, pay man to stay awake all night outside room, so I don't get kill and rob. Also need pay another man to watch flirst man in secret. Can trust no man in Lao, in city. In country, all good. I cook egg roll for all. Lao way."

"What about spaghetti for the main dish? It doesn't cost much for the food. You might make a big profit. The egg rolls will be the selling point."

"I make meatball spaghetti and ten hundred egg roll."

"The way we say that is 'one thousand.'"

"Oh, good word – soussand."

Pastor Paul's vestry and the refugee committee had become a well- oiled machine. He had a squadron of willing troops. If they were behind an idea, they came out to support it in full force. So, tickets were made, 500 of them. If people purchased advance tickets, they could save a buck. Big signs were placed around town. TOM'S LAOTIAN SPAGHETTI DINNER WITH EGG ROLLS. The tickets sold like hotcakes. The church hall was small so they had to schedule three different sittings. Tom came through on the spaghetti. Tom came through on the "soussand" egg rolls. How could one man with a couple helpers cook for 500 people? He did. Folks tipped handsomely. The church added a little more to the profit. Tom had enough money to give his parents a proper Buddhist ceremony. When he returned, he had a satisfied, contented countenance.

Because of the dinner, Tom had made many more friends

in Oak Grove. Lots of people knew who he was. Most grew to love him and accept him. He worked as the custodian at Grace Lutheran Church for several years.

9

BREAKDOWN

"TOM'S WIFE, BECKY, is here to see you," the church secretary announced to Pastor Paul. "She seems upset."

"Come on in, Becky, have a seat."

"Pastor Paul."

"What is it dear? You can tell me. I won't judge."

It was a painful silence, then tears. "It's Tom, Pastor Paul. I don't know what's wrong. He's not the same. Something is wrong."

"Take a deep breath, Becky. Take your time. Tell me. It's OK. I'm here for you." She poured out her pain.

"I don't know where to begin. Tom seems to be a different man sometimes. He came home one day with something that looked like human hair and some scraps of clothing. He made a doll. I watched as he got out a needle and thread to sew it all into what looked like a little person. One night late, I heard a noise. I snuck into the living room. There he was shoving needles into that little person, saying, 'Die, die, you son bitch. You cross me, you pay. You dirty bastard, die, die.' I snuck back to get into bed. I couldn't believe it. Isn't that Voodoo, Pastor Paul? But, that's not the worst of it, Pastor Paul. He seems to always be playing with his rifles. You know he has a couple of them. He uses them for hunting. He always brings home game for us to eat. I can't watch him dress the animals. It's so gory. It's disgusting.

He does it so easily. His hands and clothes are covered with blood. He doesn't seem to mind a bit. And, he's always bragging about things he did in the refugee camp, how he killed some Viet Cong. He was a big man in the camp, he says. He waves his rifles around like he's in a war, pretending there are people. He shouts, 'Bang, bang, you dead.' Then, the other day, he pointed the gun at me, Pastor Paul. I was so afraid. He said, 'You want be dead, Becky? I make you dead.' I started to cry. He just held the rifle at my head for a long time. Then, he put it down. He's changed, Pastor Paul. He doesn't seem like the man I married. He still loves me, I know. He loves our daughter. But there are just times, Pastor Paul, when he scares me so much. What should I do, Pastor Paul? What should I do?"

Pastor Paul and Becky talked for a long time. They both were bewildered. They both didn't really know what to say or do. All Pastor Paul could say was, "He's been through a lot, Becky. He's got a lot of anger to work through. I'll talk to him when the time is right. In the meantime, if something more happens, you come straight to me."

Pastor Paul waited for the right time when he and Tom could be alone in private, when things were calm. They sat down together. Pastor Paul asked, "How are things going, Tom? How are things going with you and Becky, with young Sharon?"

"Oh, all good, Pastor Paul."

"Tom, Becky came to see me some days ago. She was not happy. She shared with me some things that had happened with you two. Do you know what she was talking about with me?"

"Becky get excited too much. I play with her. Pretend. She no understand man, really. We just have fun. Sometime she laugh. Sometime she cry."

Pastor Paul waited some time before responding. "You don't want to scare her, do you, Tom? She hasn't had the kind of life you have had. Her world is small. Her experiences have been limited. Can you try to be more gentle with her, Tom? She's a woman. It's part of your job to protect her."

"I see, Pastor Paul. I be good. You no worry."

That was that. It seemed Tom understood. Possibly Pastor Paul's words sank in. Would Tom heed them? Time passed. All seemed well.

Then, a few weeks later, Tom arrived at work with some bruises. There were a couple bandages on his face. His arm was wrapped.

"What happened, Tom? What happened?"

"No big thing, Pastor Paul. I take care of them."

"What do you mean, Tom?"

"I get home from tend bar last night. Six guy wait for me by road. They start say bad things...Becky, Sharon. Say they kill me, fuck Becky, Sharon. I say want no trouble. Go home. Leave alone. They all jump me, all six. They not know I know Muay Lao. Hard fight. They look worse me. I make all them bleed good, break bones, send to La-la for long time. They all lay on ground. No more trouble those boys. Fight Tom? I break their ugly heads."

Pastor Paul was silent. If one could hear a jaw drop, his did.

Finally, he whispered, "Oh My God." Who were those men, he thought?

Were they from out of town, maybe down by the bar where Tom tended?

Would they be back? What could be the consequences? Would there be pay back?

"Do you think they'll be back?" Pastor Paul finally asked.

"You know word, 'hime-bare-ass'?"

"You mean embarrass, Tom?"

"They too 'hime-bare-ass' come trouble, no more. All friend ask them, 'What happened you?' They make up story. Car crash, some tin. They no trouble Tom no more. If do. I kill them."

"Tom, you must not say that. You can't think that. You'll get into big trouble talking that way. Please, Tom. Please. I know you've been through a lot, but try not to get angry. Walk away. Run away. Don't let bullies like that get under your skin. They're just not worth it, Tom. Please Tom, keep your temper under control."

"I be good for you, Pop. You proud Tom? He protect Becky and Sharon. That Lao way. I try, Pop, be good. No one hurt my Becky and Sharon. No one hurt. I love."

Pastor Paul didn't know what else to do. He stood up. Tom stood up. Pastor Paul walked closer, hoping that what he was about to do next would not violate or offend. He put his arms around Tom and drew him close. Tom hugged Pastor Paul as well, for some time. Pastor Paul whispered into Tom's ear, "I love you, son."

Time passed. There was no trouble from the six thugs. Life settled down. Pastor Paul sighed a deep breath of relief. He prayed daily that there would be no more fights. He prayed that Tom would be OK. Life slipped into a dull routine for several weeks. And then....

Tom approached Pastor Paul with an angry look. "I catch them. I see them."

"What's going on, Tom?" Tom carefully unfolded an ordinary sheet of paper he had withdrawn from his wallet. It had been folded six or eight times. When it was finally entirely unfolded, there was nothing but a blank piece of paper.

"You see, Pastor Paul. I catch them doing sex. That man and Becky, they doing it. You see. Right there. She doing sex that man!"

"Tom. I don't see anything. There's nothing there."

"You see, it there, Pastor Paul. That man fucking Becky! Right there. Picture of it."

At a loss for any good way to respond, Pastor Paul said, "I don't see anything on that paper. Tom, I think you might need professional help. You need to see a counselor, a psychiatrist. You've got some problems, Tom."

Tom screamed at Pastor Paul, "Fuck your counselor," and ran out of the church.

Pastor Paul went home that night and unburdened himself to Hilda. She was such a companion, such a listener. She hugged him. They prayed. They were perplexed as to how they might help. Pastor Paul put in a restless night's sleep.

The next morning at church the secretary announced, "Becky is here to see you, Pastor Paul. She looks very upset."

Pastor Paul welcomed Becky into his office, but before he could utter a word, Becky collapsed into his arms, sobbing uncontrollably. It took some time for Becky to settle down. She spoke with great effort. She revealed, so slowly. Word by word, with long pauses, the pain was revealed. "He...shot...his...gun... at...me. He...shot...his...gun...at...me."

Pastor Paul reached out to hold Becky's hand. "Tell me, Becky. Tell me what happened. You need to get this out, Becky."

"He had that look on his face last night. He was angry. I could tell.

He asked me why I was playing around with those other men, why I was having sex with those other men. I asked him, "'What men, Tom? I've been faithful to you. I haven't been with any other men.' He pulled out a folded piece of paper. It was nothing more than a folded piece of paper. But he claimed that it was a photo, a photo of me having sex with another man. There was nothing on that paper, Pastor Paul. Nothing. He grabbed his rifle while I was sitting on our bed with my back against the wall.

He shouted at me again and again. 'I kill you, Becky, then I kill bad men.

You be dead for have sex with them. I show you.' He aimed his rifle right at my head, Pastor Paul. He held the gun there for a long time. I was crying and shouting out, 'No, no, Tom. I love only you.' Then the gun went off. The shell went through the wall just a few inches from my head. I jumped up and looked him straight in the eye. 'I'm taking Sharon,' I said.

'When I come back, you'll be gone. You'll be gone or my father and my brothers will take care of you. I left with Sharon, Pastor Paul, and went to Daddy's. I was too afraid to tell him anything. I just made up a story. I said Tom was having friends over to drink and play cards. I said that they were making so much noise, we decided to come home to sleep.

"The next morning, I told my father and brothers that I wanted them all to come to our apartment to help clean up after Tom's party. When we got there, Tom was gone. He took his clothes, some personal items, his guns, and the car. There wasn't a note. Nothing. I told Daddy and my brothers the whole story. It's a good thing Tom was gone. There's no telling what they would have done to Tom. Sharon and I are going to move in with Mommy and Daddy. We can't stay in that apartment anymore, not after what happened. I'd be too afraid that he would come back. I had to tell you all this Pastor Paul, even though I knew it would break your heart. I have no idea where he went. I assume Tom is gone for good."

Pastor Paul cried, and Becky tried to console him. It was an awkward, painful time for both. They each said a few things, meaningless words, words to fill in empty spaces. They were both too dumbfounded to make any sense of it all anymore. Becky left to live with her father and mother, Guy and Tammy Johnson. Even in a small town like Oak Grove, it would be years before Pastor Paul saw Becky again.

10

INTERVAL

THE GRACE LUTHERAN Church refugee sponsorship committee, the vestry, the members, and the whole town had questions about Tom. All Pastor Paul could offer was, "I don't know. I don't know." He didn't know anything more except that Tom was gone. Period. Even his brother Lei Ai had heard nothing. He knew nothing. There had been no contact.

In the months that followed, rumors were heard around town that Tom was pushing drugs in New York City, that he had joined a gang of Laotians who trafficked women. Some responded, "What terrible rumors!" Others said that he was working in upstate New York for some export company, making lots of money. Nobody knew the truth.

There were occasional reported "sightings," as it were. Someone would say they saw him in town wearing a black leather jacket, with a gold necklace and earrings, driving a fancy car. He'd be there, then like a ghost gone again. But those who witnessed always said he brought presents for Sharon. He would see her walking home after school and give her a wrapped present. He'd tell her that he loved her very much. He said he wanted to see her more often, but his work made him live far away. It would be two or three years between visits. He never saw anybody but Sharon. He never visited any of his old friends. He never stopped by Grace Lutheran to see Pastor Paul.

Some years later, Becky married a nice young man in her father's church. The word was that they seemed happy. Yet outward appearances don't tell all the truth. Becky could never fully embrace her father's narrow theology. She would much rather have attended Pastor Paul's church, but her father would scream, "When hell freezes over." Yet, she was safe and loved in her new marriage. Her trauma with Tom was years behind her. She carried on. That's all anyone can do.

Becky's daughter, Sharon, really didn't know her father Tom at all. He left when she was just four years old. Her contact with him was just minutes each time over many years. Even with her stepfather's love and presence, there was a loss, a loneliness, an emptiness in Sharon's life. She struggled throughout high school, earning low grades, but did graduate. Sharon was a restless, unfocused young lady. She felt like Oak Grove, especially her grandfather's church, were nothing more than cages. She wanted to be a free bird and fly. Sharon wanted to get out before she got stuck forever in that "lousy church and dead-end town."

She made many announcements that she would leave someday. There were family arguments with lots of posturing. Conversations ended with family members storming off to various corners. She finally did secretly leave home one night with a small tote and some money she saved from working at the Dairy Queen. She didn't tell her parents where she was going or how they could reach her. She never told a soul where she was headed. She didn't speak a word to her friends. There was no note. She was gone. There was no way of finding her whereabouts. In the same way that her father Tom seemed to become a ghost, so too did Sharon. They vanished, disappeared. No amount of searching would bring them back.

Sharon did phone home every now and then to tell her parents not to worry, but she would never reveal where she was living. After several years, Sharon called one evening to share some news. "Mommy, Daddy, I have a baby boy. He's so beautiful."

Guy was shocked. "When did you get married? Who's the father?"

"I'm not married, Daddy. Nathan's father has flown the coop. I'm glad of it. It's just me and Nathan now. Someday I'll bring him home to meet you. You'll meet my new friend, Kenoa, too. She's from Laos, Daddy. Her name means 'the free one.' We live together." Guy handed the phone to his wife and left the room. His wife chatted with Sharon for a few minutes. Then they said their goodbyes, for another few years.

Tom never knew where Sharon was living. How could he? He was the ghost man, severing ties with everyone in Oak Grove. Nobody could have given him any information about where his daughter Sharon was living. How could anyone know? Even Becky's family didn't know. He wouldn't be able to find out anything from anybody. Tom wasn't going to talk with Becky. And he was certainly was not going anywhere near Becky's family. As time went by, there were no more ghost visits to Oak Grove.

So it was. Many who were involved and cared so deeply about Tom wondered about what went wrong. He had been so good and kind. Folks loved Tom. How could he have abandoned his family, and all those in Oak Grove who loved him? Was he nothing more than another ne'er-do-well husband and father?

Pastor Paul preached the pain. As he had dealt with so many questions about faith, life, purpose, he preached about this as well. "My beloved children, I don't know why God would allow our effort to fail. I don't know how we could have given so many hours, so much money, so many prayers, so much love to one man for him to simply walk out and leave. I don't know why he would abandon his wife and daughter. I don't know why we are all heartbroken. I don't know why God would allow this to happen. I don't know why God would turn his love aside. Is God powerful or powerless? Does God care at all?"

He continued his preaching. "I feel no comfort. Indeed, the Psalmist cries out in scripture, imploring the Almighty to save him, help him. When does God save? When does God help? I feel nothing but emptiness. Oh, how can I be your pastor to speak this way? Why do I not offer succor, healing, peace?" Pastor

Paul laid it all out before his congregation, week after week. He addressed his pain, their pain. It was raw. It was truth.

Surprisingly, nobody ever thought that he shouldn't be their pastor. Nobody ever suggested that he was unfit, that because he struggled with his faith he should be removed. Pastor Paul was a different sort. But he was real, honest, authentic. To them, that was what they wanted in a pastor. He was in misery with a congregation in misery. He felt their pain deeply because he felt his pain deeply.

Yet, he held out hope. "While there is life, there is hope," Pastor Paul would say. Perhaps God would have a final word. Perhaps if everyone just trusted more, had more faith, God would restore. Maybe God would heal. Maybe God would make what was broken, whole once more. Pastor Paul was often drawn to the story of the great flood, when Noah gathered two of every kind into the ark. When all the world seemed lost, to be drowned out of existence, Noah released a dove. Would it return to the ark? It did return, with an olive branch in its beak. The flood waters were receding. There was dry land somewhere. God would allow his creation to live once more. Noah was given signs of hope after the great flood: the olive branch and the rainbow in the sky. Maybe God would give Oak Grove some sign of hope and bring Tom home?

11

PRISON

"PASTOR PAUL. HELLO. This Dara, Lei Ai wife."

Pastor Paul was quite surprised to pick up the phone to hear who it was. It had been some time since anyone in Oak Grove had heard anything from Lei Ai and Dara. It was wonderful to hear her voice once again, especially just before Christmas.

"Dara, how wonderful to hear from you. How are you and Lei Ai doing?"

"Oh, we do good, Pastor Paul. Both still work, good job. We buy house now. Have two kids now. Channa finish high school. William, we call heim Billy. He in 11 grade. We good. Call to wish you and wife Hilda, Merry Christmas."

"That's so sweet, Dara. Thank you very much. What is Channa doing now that she's out of high school?"

"Oh, she still live home. Work at beauty shop. But she trouble. Drink too much friends. We want her move out. Get own place. She no go."

"It takes a while for kids to grow up. She'll be fine, Dara. She'll find her way."

"You heard Kahoku, Pastor Paul?"

"No, Dara, I haven't heard from Kahoku in years. Have you heard from him? How is he?"

"He in prison, Pastor Paul. He kill man."

"Oh, no. He's in prison?"

"He get fight with man. Kahoku kill heim. Kahoku bury body in trees. Run two days. He friend say better he turn heimself in. It be better. He go to police, tell police he kill man, where body be. They have trial Tom. Judge give him two jail. One he say twenty to forty years for kill man. Two he say ten to twenty years for bury body. Tom in state prison, not far you. We go visit one time."

"Oh dear, Dara, this is such sad news. I'm so sorry for you and Lei Ai. I'm so sorry for Tom. I can't believe it."

"He there two years. Try kill heimself two times. Try hang heimself. Now, no more try.

Maybe you see heim, Pastor Paul?"

"I'll certainly try, Dara. Tell Lei Ai, I'm so sorry."

"We sorry too, Pastor Paul. Good bye."

Pastor Paul couldn't help himself. He went home to see Hilda to tell her. They cried together. They prayed together. "Dear God in heaven, how can this be?"

Pastor Paul slipped down into reflective thought. Tom had murdered a man. Tom had taken a life. In war, that was one thing, but now Tom killed another man, an American. Did he lose his temper again? What happened that they fought? There were so many unanswered questions.

Pastor Paul thought about the sentencing. Forty years plus twenty years? Tom would never get out. He would die in prison. Why did the judge give him so many years? It seemed more than most who take a life usually receive. He knew an attorney in town. He asked him to look into it. Was it because Tom was a foreigner that the judge was so hard on him? The sentences were excessively severe. Not that murder can go without consequences. But, in many other situations, the guilty get far less than what Tom received. More questions plagued Pastor Paul. Did he want to see Tom in prison? What would he say? What would Tom say? Tom was now a murderer. Would Pastor Paul be safe going to the prison? Pastor Paul had never visited a prison before. He never had any cause to. His parishioners and friends would never do anything like that. He never had a reason to visit a state prison before. And, he thought about Jesus' exhortation to visit those in prison. Why would Jesus have said that? Did he mean to visit murderers also?

Pastor Paul didn't know where to begin. How does one go about visiting a person in a state prison? He discovered that it's almost as hard for somebody to get inside prison as it is for inmates to get out. He had to submit "background" papers, notarized character references. Then he had to seek Tom's permission to come visit him. After some time, Pastor Paul received a letter stating that he was on the approved visitor's list, along with twenty pages of procedure, protocol, do's and don'ts when visiting.

Pastor Paul set a date for his first visit. He drove the one and a half hours to the prison. All the way he thought about what he would say. What could he say?

He'd never seen a place like the state prison before. There was a long drive before reaching the parking lot. The entire prison was encircled with a tall earthen wall, so that no one inside could see anything but sky by looking out the windows. Prisoners would see no trees, no scenery, no buildings to give them any sense of where they were.

He found himself breathing heavily as he opened the steel door to go inside. The guards were not friendly. "Sign in." The guard tossed the clip board toward Pastor Paul. "License plate?" Pastor Paul was so nervous he couldn't remember what it was. "Go get it." Pastor Paul walked back to his car to get the plate number. "Inmate number?" Pastor Paul remembered that and wrote it down. "Go sit. I'll call your name." A half dozen others sat like zombies. No one spoke nor looked at anybody else. Pastor Paul looked straight ahead until his name was called. "Did you lock all belongings? Everything has to be put in the locker...keys, watch, wallet, cell phone, money, belt, everything metal, no coins." Pastor Paul put everything in a locker and returned with the key. "I'll keep that and give it to you when you leave. Go over there."

Pastor Paul moved toward a closet-sized room where a guard

stood. "Put your hand out like this." His hands were brushed with a small damp cloth held by tongs, then inserted before a screen. "Next!" He pointed in a direction. Pastor Paul found out later, this was to screen to see if he had traces of any illegal drugs on his hands.

"Take off your shoes. Walk through slowly." Pastor Paul obeyed.

"Over there." A third guard pointed. "Stand there." Pastor Paul stood before another giant steel door. Click, clang, bang, the door opened automatically. Pastor Paul walked down a long corridor with barred windows on both sides. To the outside, he saw barbed wire everywhere. The hallway ended before another steel door. Pastor Paul stood motionless, wondering what would happen next. Click, clang, bang, the door opened automatically where he was faced with another standing guard who pointed to a man sitting in an enclosed room behind a glass window. "Give me the paper." Pastor Paul handed a paper to him. "Put both hands down flat." That guard stamped both hands with an invisible mark which Pastor Paul would have to put under a screener on the way out. The guard gave him yet another piece of paper. "Through there." Pastor Paul waited before another steel door. Click, clang, bang. It opened. He walked into a large room with tables and chairs. He could see inmates in orange jumpsuits at tables talking with one or two others. There were maybe ten full tables. The room had a high ceiling. There were only small windows at the top some 25 feet up. At the far end of the room sat another guard. He motioned for Pastor Paul to come. "Paper?" Pastor Paul handed it to him. "You can hug him for a brief time, but always let me see your hands. Sit. He'll be out." Pastor Paul found a vacant table and sat for one hour taking in his surroundings, watching the others. Guards came in and out of the room. Conversations were whispers. At some tables they were playing cards. The walls were concrete blocks. There was a red line drawn on the floor 6 feet from the walls on all four sides of the room with words written on the floor, "NO INMATES."

Finally, Tom came through the door, handing the guard some papers. He looked around the room. He spotted Pastor Paul, then walked toward him. "Hi, Pop," he said.

Pastor Paul bit his lip. "Hi, Tom." They hugged briefly, then sat down. Before Pastor Paul could say a word, Tom started in. It was as if he needed to get it all out, off his chest, to make a confession.

"Pop, I happy you come. I need tell you. Yes, I kill man. Know I have do time for what I do. I so mess up, I try kill me two time. Then I decide for Sharon, I live. She have son, Nathan. He father black. That OK. He good son. She visit me two time. Nathan five year now. He come too. Lei Ai no come. Pastor Paul, judge too hard for me. Talk other inmate. No else get such long sentence. Too long. I live for Sharon, Nathan. Now I live for you, Pop."

Pastor Paul, in spite of all the difficult situations he had been in over

his life time of ministry, was having difficulty dealing with this. He was speechless. He didn't know what to say. He did not probe for any more details. It seemed without purpose. Pastor Paul tried to change the subject.

"Hilda and I have both been well. But we have missed seeing you.

I'm still at the church. All those on the sponsorship committee miss seeing you. I don't fish as much with you not around. Maybe we'll get to go fishing again...someday? How do they treat you, Tom?"

Tom looked around (he was always looking around), leaned in, and whispered. "Tough place to be, Pastor Paul. Never know when inmate go crazy, try to kill. Guards beat. Go to 'F' block."

"F Block?"

"Solitary, for most bad. Each block worse to "F." A...B...those inmate be good. C...D...E, not so good. F, big trouble. Guy in F, he be there long time. Maybe no get out. I in A block, best inmates. I no make trouble. I get work. I get go gym. I lift. Bench press 200 pound."

"Where do you work, Tom?"

"I get kitchen cook. Guard know I be good cook. I make meal for all guard. They have best meats, fresh food. I cook for guards. They know who Tom be." Tom whispered again, "No these dummy can say my name.

Kahoku Phatouttaxaysy come out like Kahot Pat Too...whatever. So they call me Alphabet. That OK. Stupid guard," he whispered. "Then after I cook good food for guard, I make meal for prisoner. I open bag food. Big bag food. On all bag, it say 'Not intended for human consumption.' I have cook meal from horse food, dog food. I don't know. Throw in many oil, spice. They all eat. No one try kill me yet." He smiled.

The initial meeting sped by quickly. Tom knew he couldn't talk long. He offered, "I go back now, Pop. See you again, maybe?"

"Sure, Tom, I'll be back to visit. We can write to each other." There was a brief hug. Tom disappeared behind the steel door, but not without first turning his head and smiling at Pastor Paul.

Then, Pastor Paul began the exiting, the extracting, the disentanglement from the prison...steel doors, barbed wire, gruff guards, long hallways. When he exited the prison, he took several deep breaths, gasping for air. It was as if he had been underwater, then came up for air. As he walked to the car, he fought back the impulse to weep. Instead, he was gripped with a thought. He was free! He was free to go, free to drive, free to be, free to live. Never had he been so thankful to be free. He drove home pondering Tom's incarceration. He drove home pondering his own newly felt freedom. For eight years, Pastor Paul made visits.

Tom shared that he was paid 17 cents an hour for his work as a cook. Eight hours a day at 17 cents is $6.80 a week, $353.60 a year. Out of that, Tom might buy some decent food at the commissary, but that would reduce his slim balance needed for more important things. He had to think about his own medical, dental, and vision needs. If Tom got sick, he had to pay the doctor out of his earned money. If Tom needed a prescription, he had to pay out of his own money for that as well. It was all just another of a hundred ways that prison made inmates' lives miserable. If he had a little money, he might buy some toothpaste or a candy bar. He had to buy his own paper, pen, envelope, and stamp to send a letter!

At one point Tom told Pastor Paul that his vision was going a little. He could use some reading glasses. He couldn't afford that, so Pastor Paul suggested a magnifying glass. He knew well enough that "glass" would not get into the prison, so Pastor Paul looked high and low to find a plastic magnifier. Into the mail it went for Tom, only to find out later that the guards had intercepted it and destroyed it. If anything looked at all suspicious, it was seized, then destroyed as "contraband."

It was Pastor Paul, Sharon, her son Nathan, and another old friend who visited Tom in prison. Lei Ai and Dara had visited only once. They seldom wrote letters. They didn't phone. But visits from the four seemed to keep Tom going. They all became his lifelines, his reasons for hope, to live long enough to get out of prison to be with his loved ones again.

Pastor Paul started sending money to Tom through J-Pay, an agency in Florida that puts contributed money into prisoners' accounts. At least four times each year, Pastor Paul would send $200, or $300, sometimes more, so that Tom could get some of his favorite snacks. When Tom first arrived, he bought a used 12-inch TV, but it didn't last long. Tom would never ask for anything. But after months going without television, he said he was saving up for a new one, that maybe he'd have enough money in four years. Pastor Paul gave him $400 that quarter to buy a new TV from the commissary. Tom paid back however he could. He painted watercolors for Pastor Paul and Hilda. The first to arrive by mail was of a hummingbird painted on plain paper. The colors and the detail were striking. Next, Tom wanted a photo of Pastor Paul and Hilda. A few months later, there was a pencil sketch of the two of them with a dove pictured above. Then came a detailed watercolor of one of the cabins at camp, surrounded by trees. Pastor Paul had all three framed to hang in his home.

With the little extra money he had, Tom decided to buy supplies to write his memories in the Lao language. He figured that someday, it might be translated into English by someone skilled in both languages. He had written about a hundred pages. He wanted to someday pass it on to Sharon and Nathan. There was a shake down, as there periodically was. Guards stormed into each cell, tossing mattresses on the floor, throwing clothes, reading mail.

"What's this?" a guard demanded, holding up the pages of Tom's memoirs.

"That my book. I want give to daughter Sharon." "Book? Shit. That's contraband." They ripped up the pages in front of him, then threw them in a trash bin.

On one visit, Tom told Pastor Paul he had been assigned to a new job. They didn't want him as cook anymore. The prison was being cut financially. They could no longer afford the good food for the guards. Cuts were being made everywhere. Tom said there were some days they didn't have lights. Sometimes the water was shut off for hours. On days when there was no heat, Tom had to pile up every piece of clothing he had on his bed and crawl under to stay warm. Tom's new job was unloading trucks...laundry, supplies, equipment. After six years working, they raised his hourly rate from 17 cents to 18 cents per hour.

Tom asked Pastor Paul if he could look into his sentencing, if there were any way for a retrial, any way his sentence could be reduced. Pastor Paul did what he could. He wrote letters. He wrote dozens of letters over the years. He wrote to the head of the prison, to lawyers, to state representatives, to the governor, to congressmen, to the United States President. Not once did he receive a response from anyone. He contacted everyone he thought who might be able to help. Everywhere he turned, it was a dead-end. There was simply no possibility of changing anything related to his sentencing.

In spite of all the discouraging news each time Pastor Paul came to visit, he was always greeted with a hug and a "Hi, Pop. How you doing?"

Tom was always happy to see his Pop to chat about this and that. They especially enjoyed re-living their times fishing, dreaming of having a

restaurant together. At times, Pastor Paul had second thoughts about bringing up such topics. But he could see the joy in Tom's eyes as they remembered the old days. What fun they had! When they would end their conversation, as Pastor Paul gave his hug and was about to leave, Tom would always say, "See you next time. I going nowhere."

12

COVID

"**PASTOR PAUL. THIS** is Sharon. Daddy is in the hospital with Covid."

"Oh dear. Oh no. What are the details, Sharon?"

"They took him in about three days ago. He was already bad. Of course, none of the prisoners had been vaccinated. None of the prisoners were issued masks. Pastor Paul, I hate to put it this way, but those poor men in prison are nothing more than rats in a trap, waiting to be drowned. I was called by the prison. They told me he had been taken to Our Lady of Mercy Hospital. I had to make arrangements for Nathan, so I couldn't come until yesterday. There are two guards outside his room. I'm the only one they are letting in. Pastor Paul. He's real bad. He's on a ventilator. He's gasping for air. He keeps asking to see you, Pastor Paul. He keeps saying over and over again that he wants to see his Pop. What can we do, Pastor Paul?"

"We can pray, Sharon. We'll do just that. I'll get the church's prayer chain going. God hears our prayers, Sharon. But what about you?

Where are you staying? Do you need money? How long will you be staying near the hospital?"

"I'm OK, Pastor Paul. I found a cheap motel nearby. I have enough money. I just can't stop crying, Pastor Paul. I feel so helpless. Daddy keeps calling out for you. Can you come? I know it would mean the world to him if you could come, Pastor Paul. I think you know I haven't seen Daddy or Mommy in years. I've had no contact with my brothers. My wife Kenoa just can't get away from her job. I feel so alone."

"Your daddy told me you'd found someone to love. I'm so happy for you, Sharon. Tom is so proud of you. He's happy about you and Kenoa. And, well… Nathan? You never saw a grandpa so proud of his grandson. How Tom would talk about him when I came for visits. Sharon, we're just going to take this step by step. Let me make some phone calls. In the meantime, just do this. Sit there with your dad. Hold his hand. Tell him again and again that you love him. Tell him I love him. Tell him I'll be there to see him soon. Tell him he's a tough old fisherman, that I want to fish with him again. Thank him for being your father. Tell him all good things, and pray. God will give you strength. I'll be in touch as I can. Your dad loves you. I love you, Sharon. Goodbye for now."

In the next minute, Pastor Paul was on the phone to Our Lady of Mercy Hospital. "This is Pastor Paul of Grace Lutheran Church in Oak Grove. Put me through to Kahoku Phaouttaxaysy's room please."

There was a long pause. "We can't do that Pastor."

"Listen, I know he's a prisoner, but I'm his pastor. He surely has a phone in his room. I am requesting that I speak with him on the phone."

"He is to have no contact with anyone but his daughter."

"For heaven's sake. How can this be right? Who can I talk to? Put me through to the guards."

"There is no phone. They will not speak to you."

"Who, then, can I talk with? I just want to pray with the man on the phone. For God's sake. You are the Lady of Mercy Hospital. Can't you do something?"

"We have been given our instructions, sir. I'm sorry, there is nothing we can do for you. We are under strict Covid protocol."

Pastor Paul was confounded. He threw several books against the wall, then pounded his fist upon his desk. He heard himself blurting out a stream of colorful words he was not used to speaking. What would he tell Sharon? What could he do?

Later that day, Sharon called. "He's taken a turn for the worse, Pastor Paul. He keeps calling out for you. That's all he says. He wants to see his Pop. Over and over, he says, 'I want to see my Pop.'"

"Sharon, they won't even let me talk with him on the phone. If I came, they wouldn't let me in. I'm so sorry, Sharon. I'd move heaven and earth to be there. You know that. If there were any way."

Pastor Paul couldn't help himself. He started to sob. Sharon joined in. Words seemed useless in that moment. They were overcome, overwhelmed. Neither was in control of anything, least of all their emotions.

Finally, Pastor Paul squeezed out the words, "Sharon, you have to be there for me. Pretend to be me. He may believe that I am there. Be his daughter. Be his Pop. Be all love to sustain him in this moment."

Pastor Paul tossed and turned all night. There would be no restful sleep for him. His mind raced. He imagined Tom in the hospital bed calling out to him over and again. Pastor Paul could not respond to his need. What kind of pastor was he? He thought of himself as a failure, a sham, a lame excuse for a minister. After all, he was the representative of a powerless God. Pastor Paul could do nothing. His God did do nothing.

Shortly after 8 a.m. the next day, the telephone rang. Pastor Paul couldn't move toward the phone. He sat there. Hilda inquired, "Should I answer the phone, dear?" He said nothing. She picked up the receiver.

"It's Sharon, dear. You should speak with her." Pastor Paul stumbled toward the phone. His hands were literally shaking.

"Daddy died, Pastor Paul."

"I know," he responded.

"It's over, Pastor Paul. I was with him until the end. I've never been with someone dying before. He finally settled down. He seemed to be sleeping. Then he just stopped breathing. Like that, he was gone. We were there for him, Pastor Paul, both you and me. He knew you were at his bedside. He knew. Don't feel bad, Pastor Paul. Daddy is at peace now. No one can hurt him anymore."

"We'll be in touch, Sharon." Pastor Paul sank into his chair.

Hilda brought him a cup of coffee and shared, "I was out on my morning walk today. The sun was just coming up. I saw an eagle. I never see eagles on my early morning walks. At that moment, I knew that Tom had died. His spirit was in the eagle. He was soaring, free. You did everything you could, dear. His soul is now in the hands of our Lord."

13

CONSOLATION

PASTOR PAUL STRAUSSER stepped into the pulpit on his last Sunday at the Grace Lutheran Church in Oak Grove. He was a much older man than his years. He was worn out. He wanted to step away from ministry before he became another old doddering pastor. He didn't want to be remembered as fumbling his way through a sermon, forgetting his thoughts, an embarrassment to everyone, including himself. He wanted to leave on a high note, if there were such a thing.

His congregation had grown, slightly. He commented many times about his faithful members, "Why do you folks come to hear me, Sunday after Sunday? I've run out of things to say, yet you're here." Nobody would ever answer his questions. Perhaps, even after all the years in professional ministry, he didn't understand that it was his presence that was most important, not fancy words in sermons. He had been with his flock in joy and sorrow, at their weddings, with them in sickness and trouble. And, most importantly, he was there to bury their loved ones. It is a powerful ministry to walk through the valley of the shadow of death with someone in need. All the way to the cemeteries and afterwards, Pastor Paul stood by their side. Often with no words to share, he was with them all the way in his ministry of "presence."

Pastor Paul's wife, Hilda, was always there to support him

as well. Without her, there would have been no ministry. She was his silent sounding board to field all his frustrations, all his pain, all his disappointments. Her strength was his strength. While their marriage was strong, there was always that empty space, a seat set at the table, not for Elijah, but for the son or daughter that never was. Then Tom came to Grace Lutheran and into Pastor Paul's life. Oh, what a blessing! They say that people come into our lives "for a reason or a season." Tom was with them for a season. That they knew. Yet, what was the reason? How did any of his story make any sense?

Ministry had taken a physical toll. Had it taken a spiritual toll as well? He was still the Paul Strausser with more questions than answers. He was still the Paul Strausser who described the world, not in blacks and whites, but in shades of gray. There always seemed to be fine lines between joy and sorrow, fulfillment and hunger, peace and a raging war within.

He was never inauthentic with his flock. He was as real as real could be. Maybe his opinions and ideas were not "the truth," but they were his truth. He lived Abraham Lincoln's words: "I have planted myself upon the truth and the truth only, so, as far as I knew it or could be brought to know it." He understood his life and purpose in this creation only as God revealed it to him. Though he yo-yoed from doubt to faith a hundred times each day, he still offered his prayers, he still reached out his hand into the unknown in the hope that God would be there.

So, he began his last sermon at Grace Lutheran with these words. "My beloved children, we have journeyed together in faith over mountains, through valleys. We have been with each other on our pilgrimage toward God.

"Today's topic is 'consolation.' What does it mean to be consoled? We offer consolation during difficult times of life: sickness, loss, death. Does it change anything? Does it help? Does holding the hand of someone who has lost a loved one in death, saying 'I'm sorry for your loss' mean anything at all? Does it help the grieving? Does it lift their burden? We can't bring their loved one back from death. Does consolation really change anything?

"When I think back over the loses in my life, you have all offered your consolation. As you and I reflect back over those awful times, did being with each other make any difference? I think it did. I think it does make a difference. In some small ways, our efforts are not in vain. When our loved one died, when dozens of family and friends came to calling hours or the service, how did we feel? I'll tell the magic. Each person who came took back with them just a little bit of the pain and loss. So together, from the mutual love of community, you and I have received consolation, a lessening of our pain. God does work through us, my friends, in ways we may not fully understand. God expresses his unity with us through our minds and hands and love. I thank you, my beloved community of faith, that we have been consolation to each other."

After the closing hymn, he went down the aisle to offer final benediction, and words from St. Augustine. "I do believe, my children, but 'my soul is restless until it finds its rest with thee.' Amen." Offering that, it was over. Those were Pastor Paul's last official words to his congregation. There was a pleasant time of fellowship after worship. He graciously received the gift of a wall clock that chimed. He cleaned out his desk, packed up his books, turned in his keys, and left. Decades of ministry were over.

Pastor Paul went home feeling like he was in free fall over a cliff. What would he do next? What does "retirement" mean? Weeks passed. Months passed. He felt like he was wandering the wilderness. What was his purpose in life now?

Just after Easter the following year, a new family moved in next door to Pastor Paul and Hilda. The Straussers had heard about a massive Afghan resettlement with many US communities joining in the effort to receive those displaced by the Taliban. Could this be one of the families? Quick looks revealed that they were darker-skinned.

"We'll take them some cookies," Hilda announced to Pastor Paul.

They both went over the next day to introduce themselves. "I am Pastor Paul Strausser. This is my wife, Hilda. Do you speak English?"

"Oh, yes, quite well, I think. My husband was a translator for the American soldiers stationed In Afghanistan."

"Well, then, that should make our getting to know one another a lot easier. Please receive these cookies. Welcome to America. Welcome to Oak Grove. We have a lovely front porch to sit on. Perhaps you and your family will come over to chat one day soon?"

The woman responded, "That would be lovely indeed. My name is Fatanah, Fatanah Wardok. We'll see you later then."

Both Pastor Paul and Hilda were very excited about their new neighbors. Perhaps they would become good neighbors, good friends. They waited for a few days until the spring temperatures were quite warm to sit on the porch and chat. Fatanah came with two boys.

"Is Mr. Wardok working today?" Pastor Paul asked innocently.

"Well, no, Pastor Paul. I am a widow. The Taliban killed my husband Jahid nearly two years ago."

"Oh, forgive me, Fatanah. I'm so sorry."

"You could not know, Pastor Paul. Don't feel badly. I miss Jahid every day. But had he not died, we might not have been selected to come to America where we will be safe."

Conversation went quickly as both families were sharing and learning about each of their pasts. The Wardoks lived in Jalalabad. They had early exposure to good education, English, and Americans. Even though Afghanistan is 99% Muslim and less than 1% Christian, they embraced the Christian faith. Both of their sons were baptized with Christian names. The Straussers were eagerly learning, and Fatanah was happy to share. Their language was Pashto. The name for mother, they learned, was Abay and for father, Plar. They learned that many of the Afghan foods are similar to what Americans eat, although they do eat lots of mutton and rice. Their New Year's Day is March 21, which surprised both Pastor Paul and Hilda. They learned that

Afghans love poetry, that they are a proud people who enjoy music and dance. It was a lovely afternoon of sharing.

The two boys were well behaved, having their cookies and milk and reading books while the adults talked. "Tell us about your sons, Fatanah."

"My youngest here is James Michael. He is four years old. He does not remember his father [she whispered]. And this is my nine year old, Thomas Peter. He's becoming a handful. He needs a man's guidance."

"Well, I've always said, Fatanah, that it takes some time for kids to grow up, but they usually turn out just fine. Maybe Thomas would like to come over another day and have a cola with me."

Thomas chimed right in, "Abay, Abay, I want Pepsi-Cola. Can I come over, Abay? Can I?"

"You do your studies and chores around the house, and I'm sure you can."

On another front-porch spring-day, Pastor Paul phoned Fatanah to ask if it would be OK for Thomas to come over for the promised soft drink. Pastor Paul could hear Thomas in the background begging, "Please, Abay. Please." Fatanah gave her consent. Thomas and Pastor Paul were shortly sitting on his porch together enjoying some cola on ice.

"How do you like living in Oak Grove, Thomas? Do you like your school? What is new to you about America?"

"America is different. And, America is the same. Everything is so green here. Your houses are made from wood. Our houses are adobe clay. The kids in school are nice enough, but no one looks like me. I have made two friends already, Billy and Kevin. Their homes are down the street."

"What is that in your pocket, Thomas? Is that a toy?"

Thomas pulled out a sling shot from his back pocket, then proudly announced, "It's mine."

"Oh, a sling shot. What do you do with that?"

"I'll show you." Thomas asked Pastor Paul if he could have the empty cola can, which he set up on the railing at the far end of the porch. Then he went to the other side, pulled out a smooth stone and loaded up. Snap. Clink. He knocked the can off the railing at 25 feet. "Back home I would kill the scorpions and spiders."

"Well, you are quite the marksman and protector."

"I'm the man in the family now that my plar has gone to be with Jesus in heaven."

"That's a very sad thing that your father has died. I'm sure he loved you and your mother and brother very much.Our faith in Jesus gives us hope and helps us to live bravely."

They both sat with their heads slightly drooped in silent reflection. Then each began looking upon the springtime blossoms and budding trees.

"I was just wondering, Thomas. Do you like to fish?" Do they have fish in your home country?"

"Oh, yes. I went fishing many times with Plar. We would catch longasa, osman, and loach, from the Kabul River."

"Did you shore fish?"

"Yes, we didn't have a boat."

"I have a small boat, Thomas. Would you like to ride in my boat someday?"

Thomas started bobbing up and down on his chair like a jumping bean. "Would we go fishing, too?"

"We surely will, Thomas. You and I will fish together. We'll catch many fish together. We'll talk and share stories."

Both finished their colas. Thomas started walking toward his home. He turned his head and smiled at Pastor Paul. It was a fine spring day in Oak Grove.

QUESTIONS FOR REFLECTION AND DISCUSSION

There are many ideas or themes introduced in the book TOM.

What happens to those in the aftermath of war?

Why do some people accept strangers and other fear them?

Was America helping or hurting Laos during the Vietnam conflict?

What prompts some people to help others?

What is your concept of a good pastor?

What is your concept of a good marriage?

How do we protect our loved ones?

Do you think that prisons are as they were described in the book?

Does prayer make any difference?

Does God comfort and console us?

Is life destiny or lottery?

Is there an equality or inequality to life?

How do people acquire faith?

What are the foundations of hope?

Are people good or bad?

What do you think is the overall point of or message of this book?

CPSIA information can be obtained
at www.ICGtesting.com
Printed in the USA
BVHW040554230322
632147BV00004B/51

9 781977 252210